EDE/cm

D0835487

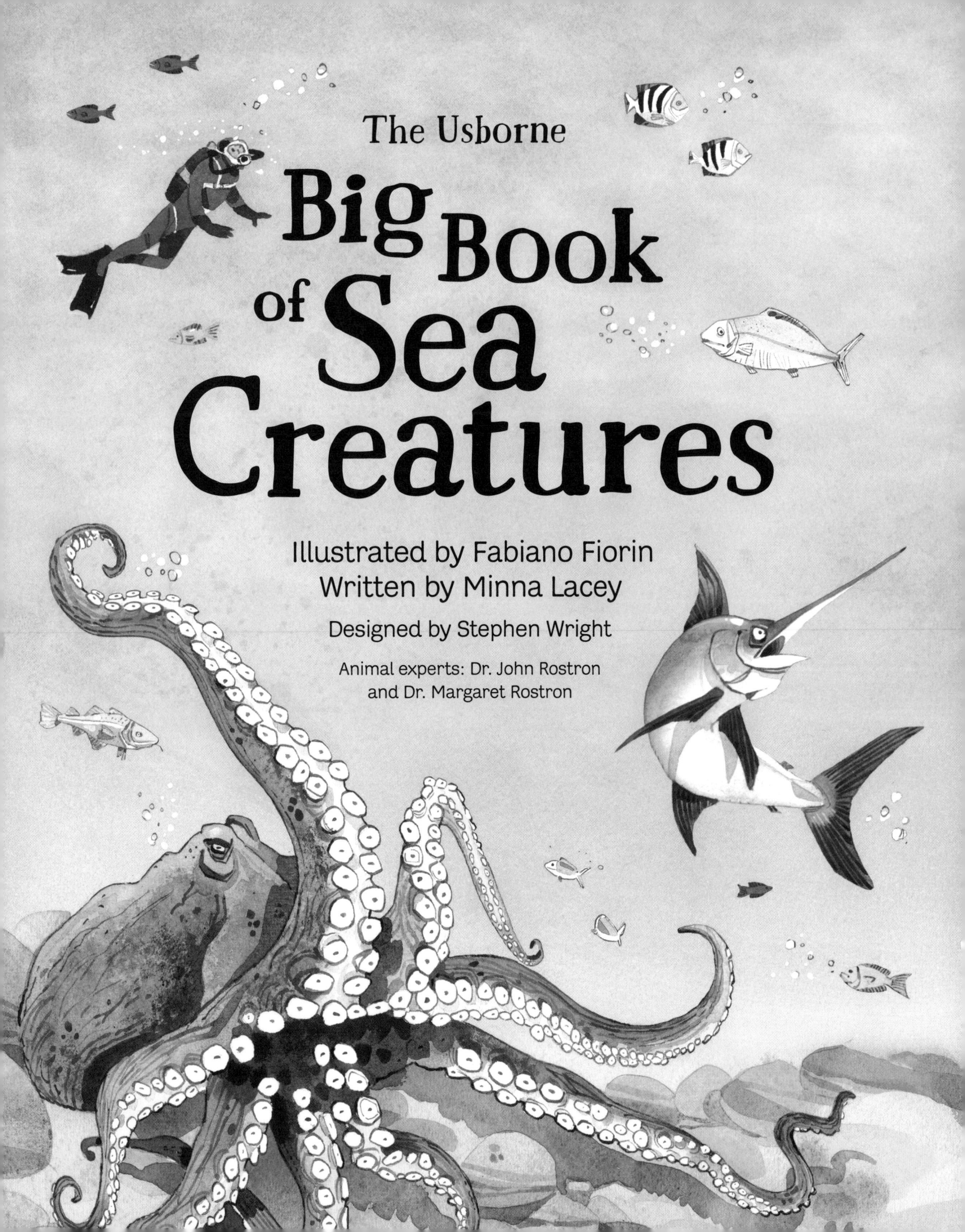

The Usborne

Big Book of Sea Creatures

Illustrated by Fabiano Fiorin
Written by Minna Lacey
Designed by Stephen Wright
Animal experts: Dr. John Rostron
and Dr. Margaret Rostron

Coral reef

A coral reef is home to all sorts of amazing sea creatures. It is made from the skeletons of lots of tiny animals and takes thousands of years to grow.

This GIANT **manta ray** sometimes leaps high out of the water. A fully grown ray can reach a massive 7m (23ft) in width.
Emperor angelfish
It uses these mouth flaps to gather up tiny animals and plants to eat.
A **giant barrel sponge** can live for more than 1,000 years. This one is taller than a man.
Sea cucumbers crawl slowly along the reef grabbing food with their sticky tentacles.

Blue whales usually come to the surface to breathe every four minutes. But when diving for food they can stay beneath the water for 30 minutes.
Atlantic walruses feed mostly on shellfish. They can suck the soft flesh out of shells in a few seconds.
Bottlenose dolphins make whistling and clicking noises to send signals to each other.

Killer whales have the largest dorsal fins of any whale or dolphin. Some fins grow 2m (6ft) high – as tall as a man.
A **humpback whale** is a powerful swimmer that often leaps out of the water.
Animals called barnacles grow on its skin.

Mammals

Some of the biggest and most extraordinary animals in the sea are vast mammals that swim and hunt underwater but come to the surface to breathe.

South American sea lions hunt for fish, squid and small penguins close to the shore.

Length: over 2½m (8ft)

Lift the pages to see ocean mammals drawn roughly to scale.

Steller's sea lion males have a thick neck and hairy mane, like a lion.

Length: about 3m (10ft)

Atlantic walruses use their tusks for fighting and hauling themselves onto the Arctic ice.

Length: up to 3m (10ft)

Killer whales are the largest kind of dolphin.

Length: up to 10m (33ft)

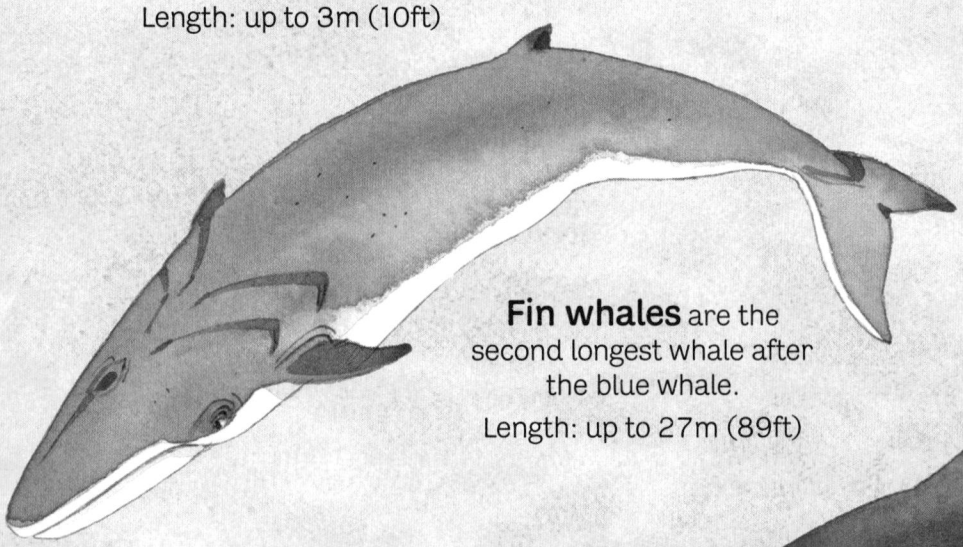

Fin whales are the second longest whale after the blue whale.

Length: up to 27m (89ft)

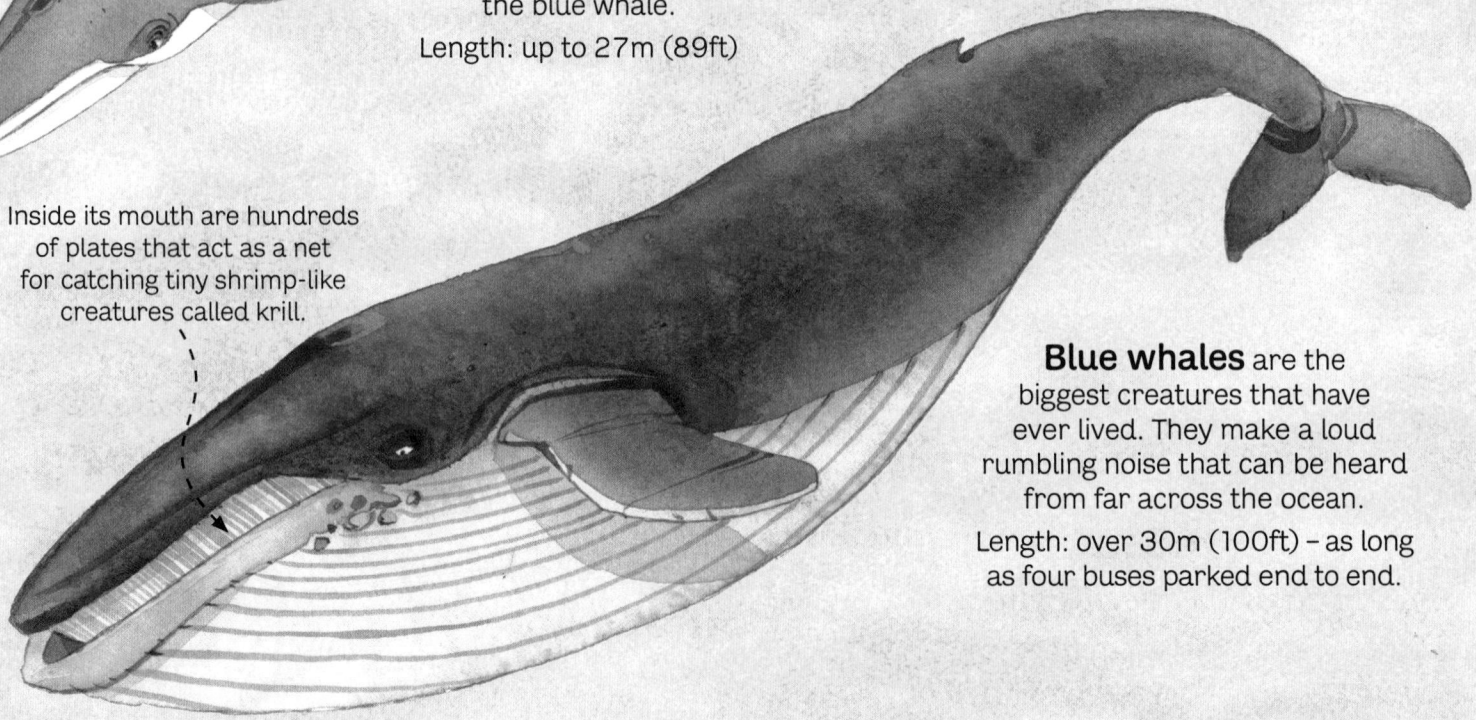

Inside its mouth are hundreds of plates that act as a net for catching tiny shrimp-like creatures called krill.

Blue whales are the biggest creatures that have ever lived. They make a loud rumbling noise that can be heard from far across the ocean.

Length: over 30m (100ft) – as long as four buses parked end to end.

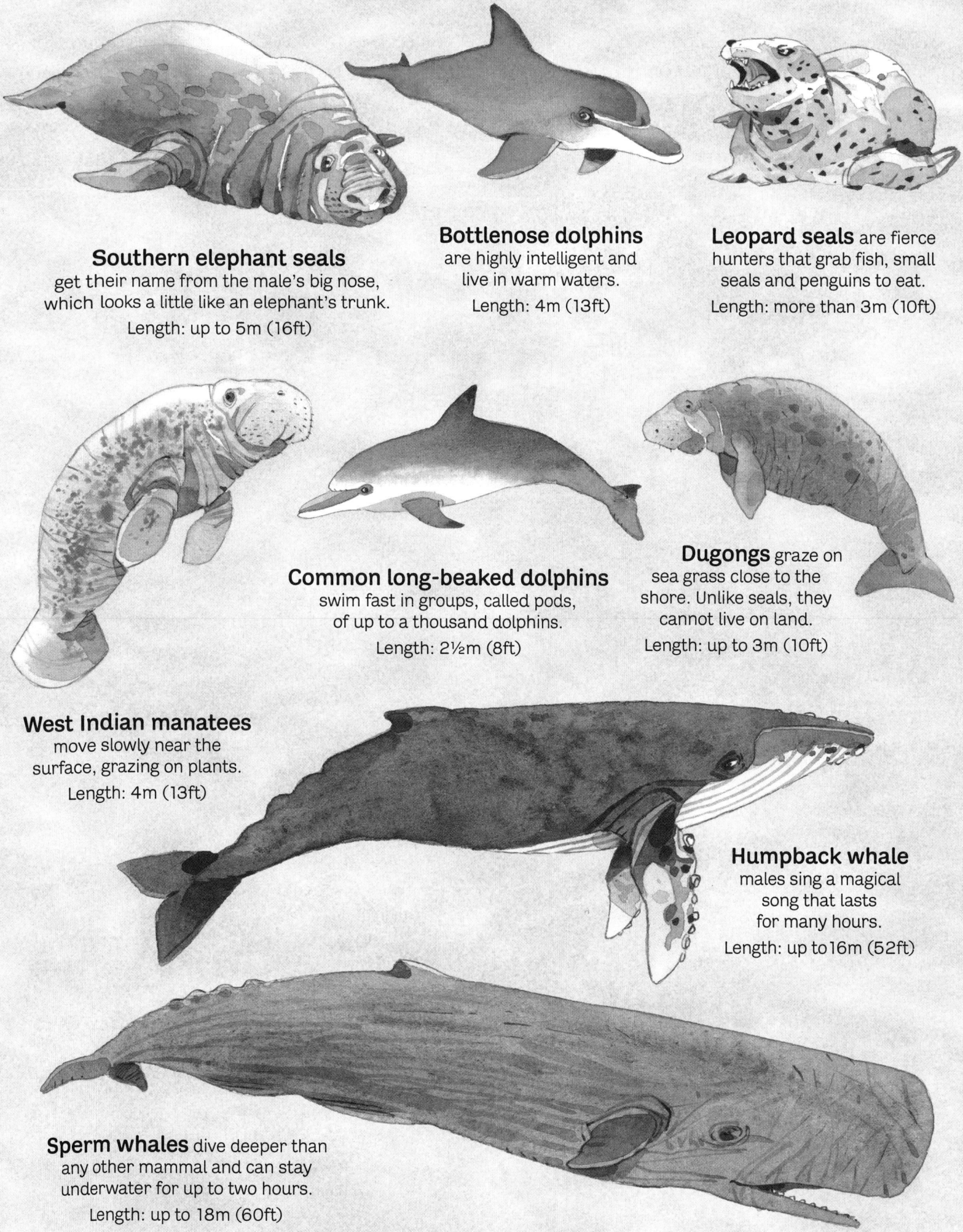

Southern elephant seals get their name from the male's big nose, which looks a little like an elephant's trunk.
Length: up to 5m (16ft)

Bottlenose dolphins are highly intelligent and live in warm waters.
Length: 4m (13ft)

Leopard seals are fierce hunters that grab fish, small seals and penguins to eat.
Length: more than 3m (10ft)

Common long-beaked dolphins swim fast in groups, called pods, of up to a thousand dolphins.
Length: 2½m (8ft)

Dugongs graze on sea grass close to the shore. Unlike seals, they cannot live on land.
Length: up to 3m (10ft)

West Indian manatees move slowly near the surface, grazing on plants.
Length: 4m (13ft)

Humpback whale males sing a magical song that lasts for many hours.
Length: up to16m (52ft)

Sperm whales dive deeper than any other mammal and can stay underwater for up to two hours.
Length: up to 18m (60ft)

Sperm whales are the biggest hunters in the ocean. They often attack giant squid deep below the surface.
Blue whales breathe through two blow holes on top of their head.

Male **southern elephant seals** fight and roar loudly to defend a piece of land. They can live without food for three months while guarding a space.
Leopard seals take their name from the black spots on their fur.
Sea lions often hunt in groups for fish, squid, octopuses and crabs.

Octopuses, squid & jellyfish

Octopuses, squid and jellyfish have soft bodies and no shell. They have writhing arms or poisonous tentacles to help them catch prey.

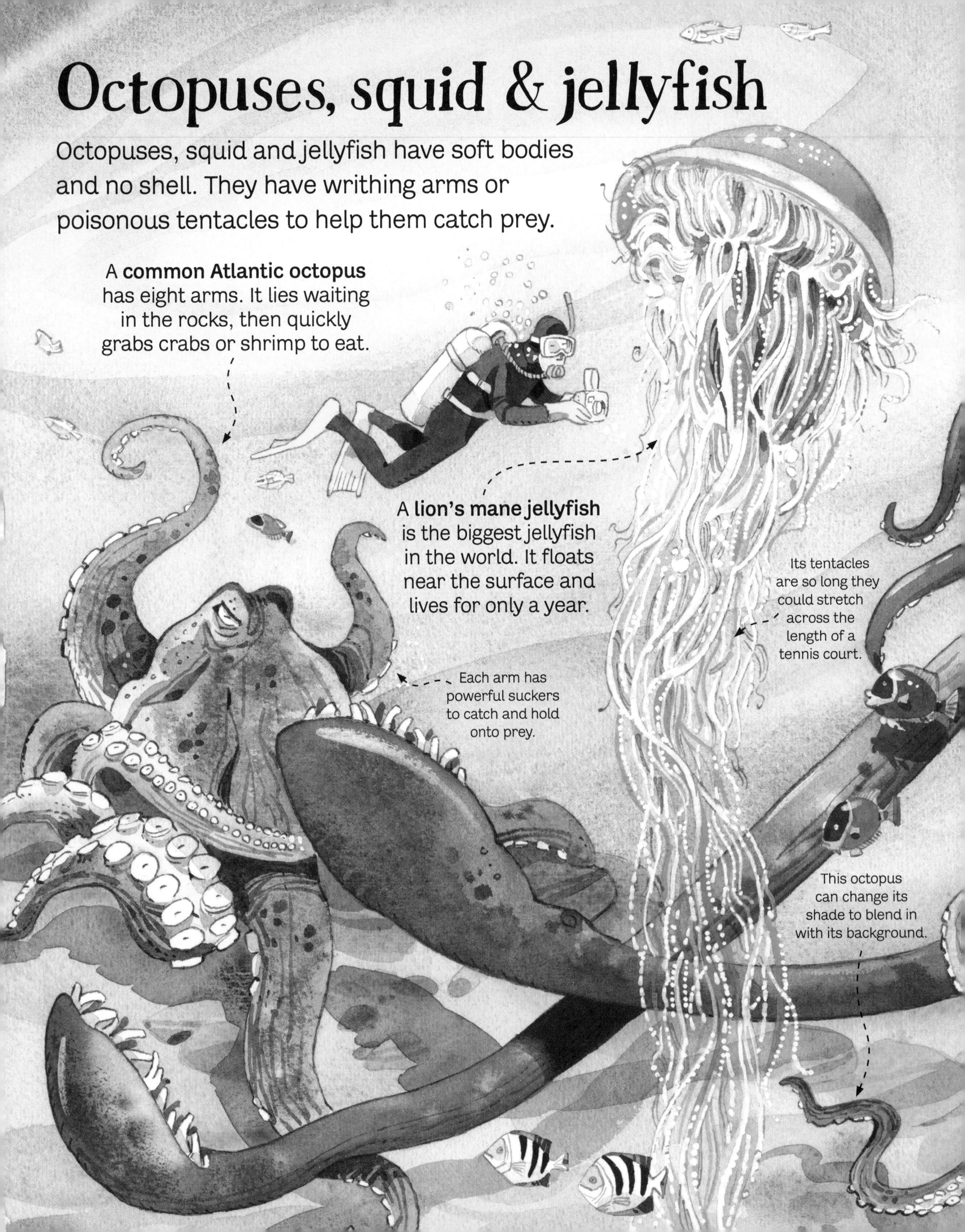

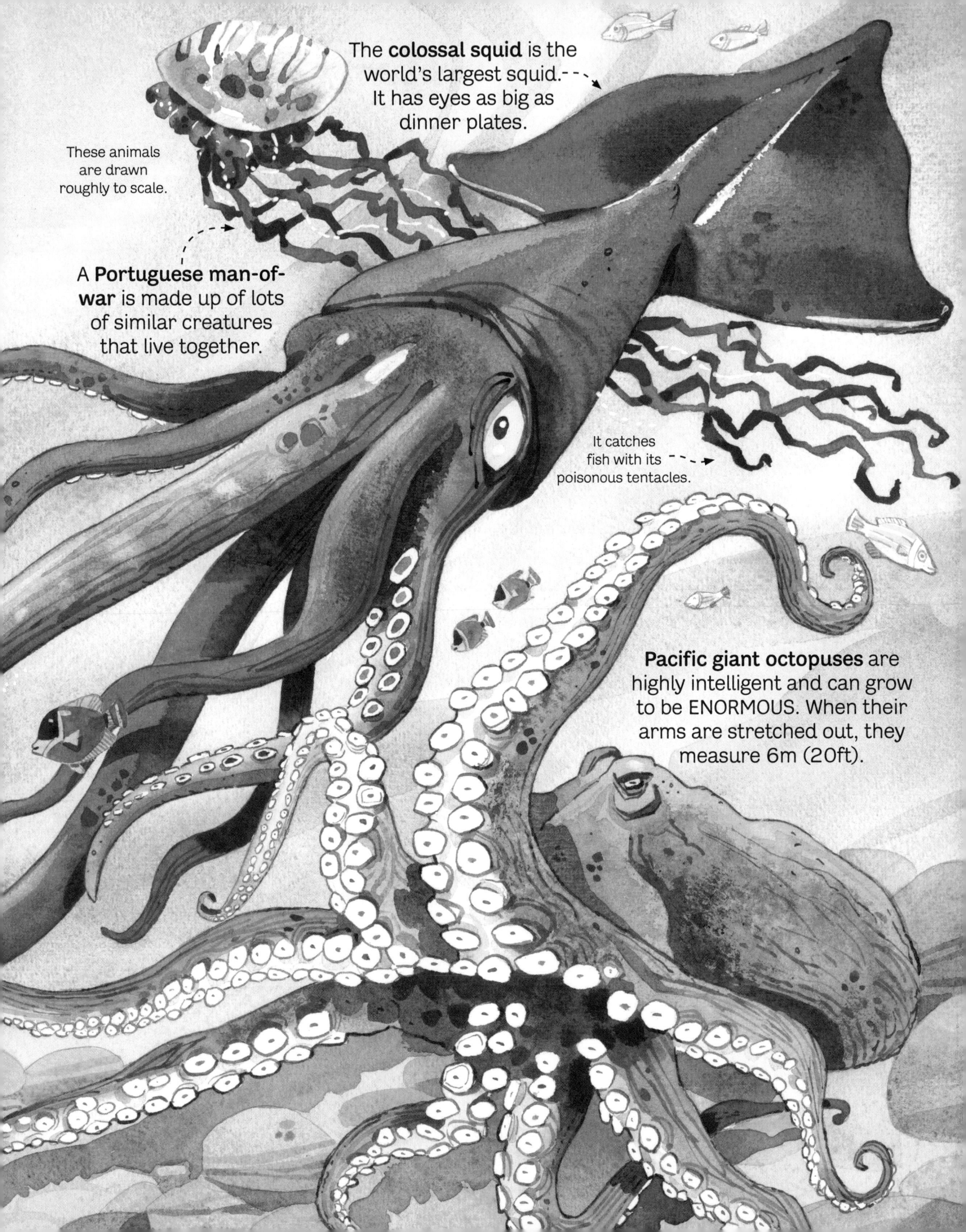
The **colossal squid** is the world's largest squid. It has eyes as big as dinner plates.
These animals are drawn roughly to scale.
A **Portuguese man-of-war** is made up of lots of similar creatures that live together.
It catches fish with its poisonous tentacles.
Pacific giant octopuses are highly intelligent and can grow to be ENORMOUS. When their arms are stretched out, they measure 6m (20ft).

Animals with shells

Many sea creatures have soft bodies with hard shells or bony skeletons on the outside, to give them protection from hungry predators.

All sea turtles have a shell on their backs – except the **leatherback sea turtle**, which has a tough, leathery skin instead.

This is the clam's mouth. It uses it to suck up tiny animals called plankton.

A **giant clam** has a huge shell with four or five folds in it. It can live for 100 years and stays in the same place all its life.

This bluish shade is produced by plants called algae that live on the clam.

The **emperor nautilus** has a striking brown and white shell with many compartments inside. It swims along by sucking in and shooting out jets of water.

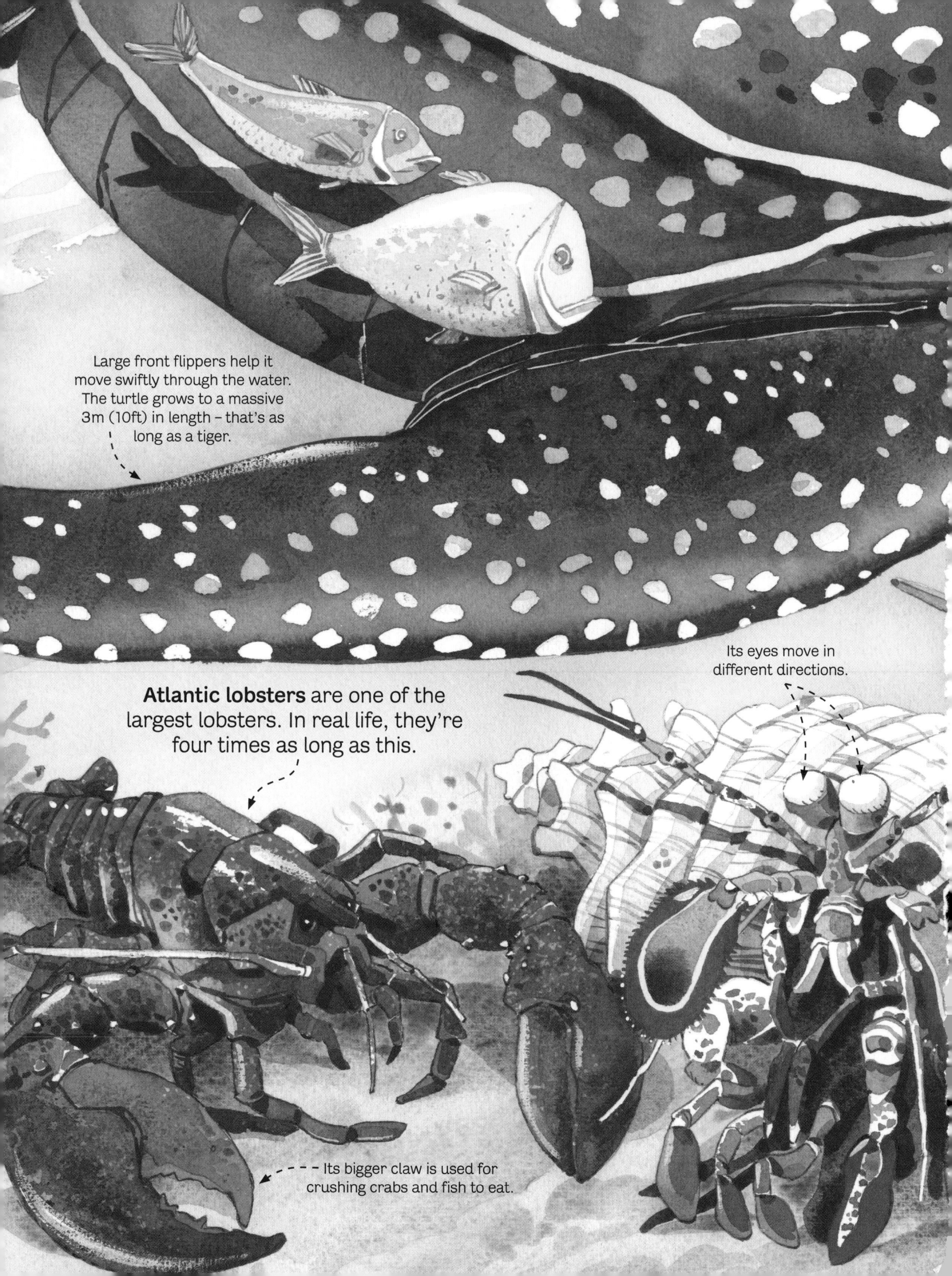
Large front flippers help it move swiftly through the water. The turtle grows to a massive 3m (10ft) in length – that's as long as a tiger.
Its eyes move in different directions.
Atlantic lobsters are one of the largest lobsters. In real life, they're four times as long as this.
Its bigger claw is used for crushing crabs and fish to eat.

A **blue shark** has a slender body and is blue on top. It feeds on schools of fish and squid.
These **horse-eye jacks** are no bigger than rabbits.
A **goblin shark** is pink with a strange beak-like snout. It lives in deep, dark waters.

A **whale shark** is the biggest kind of fish. It has no teeth and grows to a massive 14m (46ft) – that's longer than a bus.
Sharks breathe through these gill slits.
A fully grown **epaulette shark** has a large black spot on its shoulder.

This **horse conch** is a large snail with a soft body and a hard shell to hide in. It hunts whelks and oysters.
A **horseshoe crab** lives on the sea floor. As it gets bigger, it sheds its old shell then starts growing a new one.
The **mantis shrimp** likes to hide in burrows in the sand. It stabs prey with its sharp claws.
Red hermit crabs live inside empty snail shells. As they grow, they look for bigger shells to move into.

This **Japanese spider crab** has extremely long legs that stretch 4m (13ft) from claw to claw. It feeds on shellfish and can live for 100 years.
Even its body is the size of a basketball.
This **giant triton** shell is twice as big as a motorcycle helmet.

Sharks

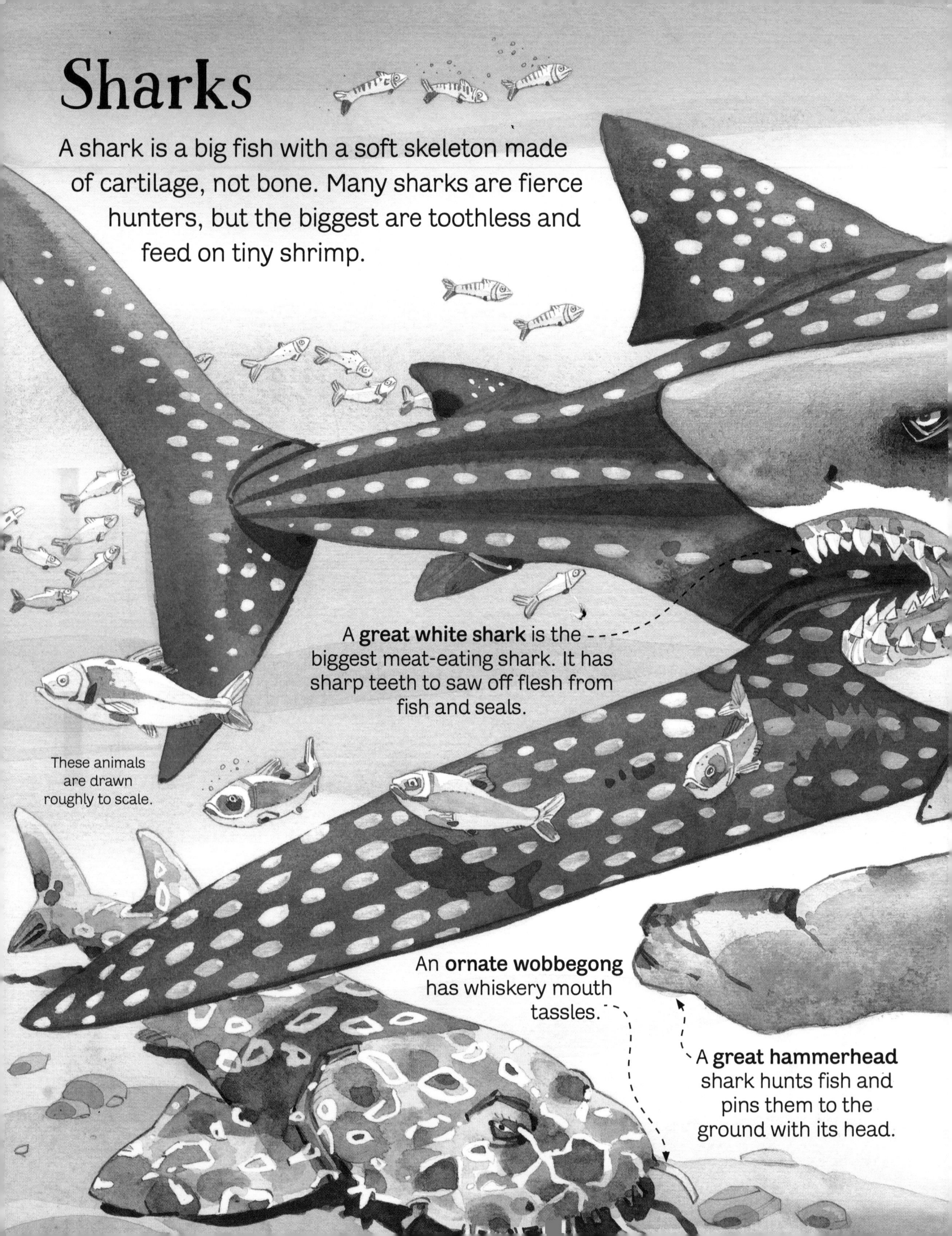
A shark is a big fish with a soft skeleton made of cartilage, not bone. Many sharks are fierce hunters, but the biggest are toothless and feed on tiny shrimp.
A **great white shark** is the biggest meat-eating shark. It has sharp teeth to saw off flesh from fish and seals.
These animals are drawn roughly to scale.
An **ornate wobbegong** has whiskery mouth tassles.
A **great hammerhead** shark hunts fish and pins them to the ground with its head.

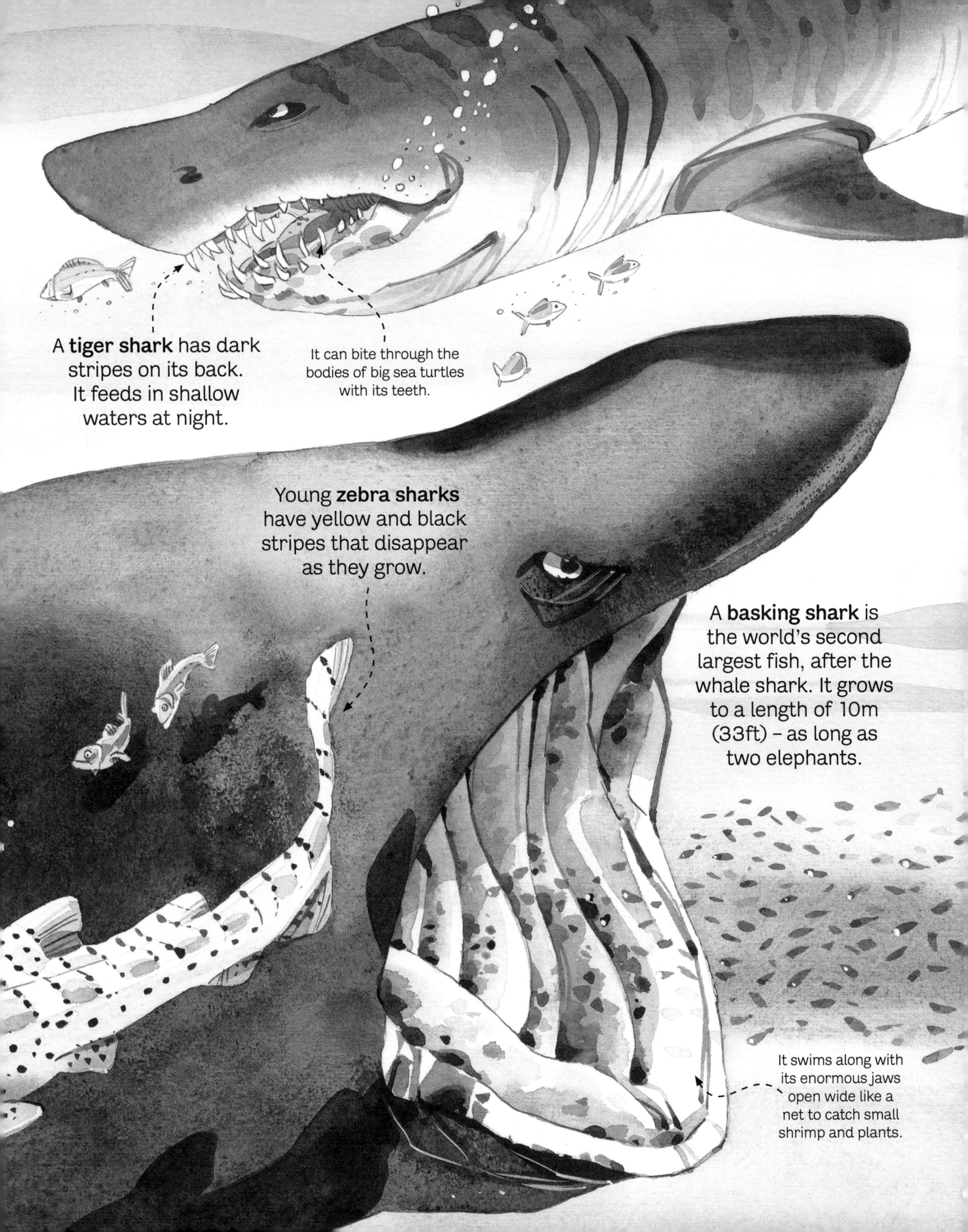
A **tiger shark** has dark stripes on its back. It feeds in shallow waters at night.
It can bite through the bodies of big sea turtles with its teeth.
Young **zebra sharks** have yellow and black stripes that disappear as they grow.
A **basking shark** is the world's second largest fish, after the whale shark. It grows to a length of 10m (33ft) – as long as two elephants.
It swims along with its enormous jaws open wide like a net to catch small shrimp and plants.

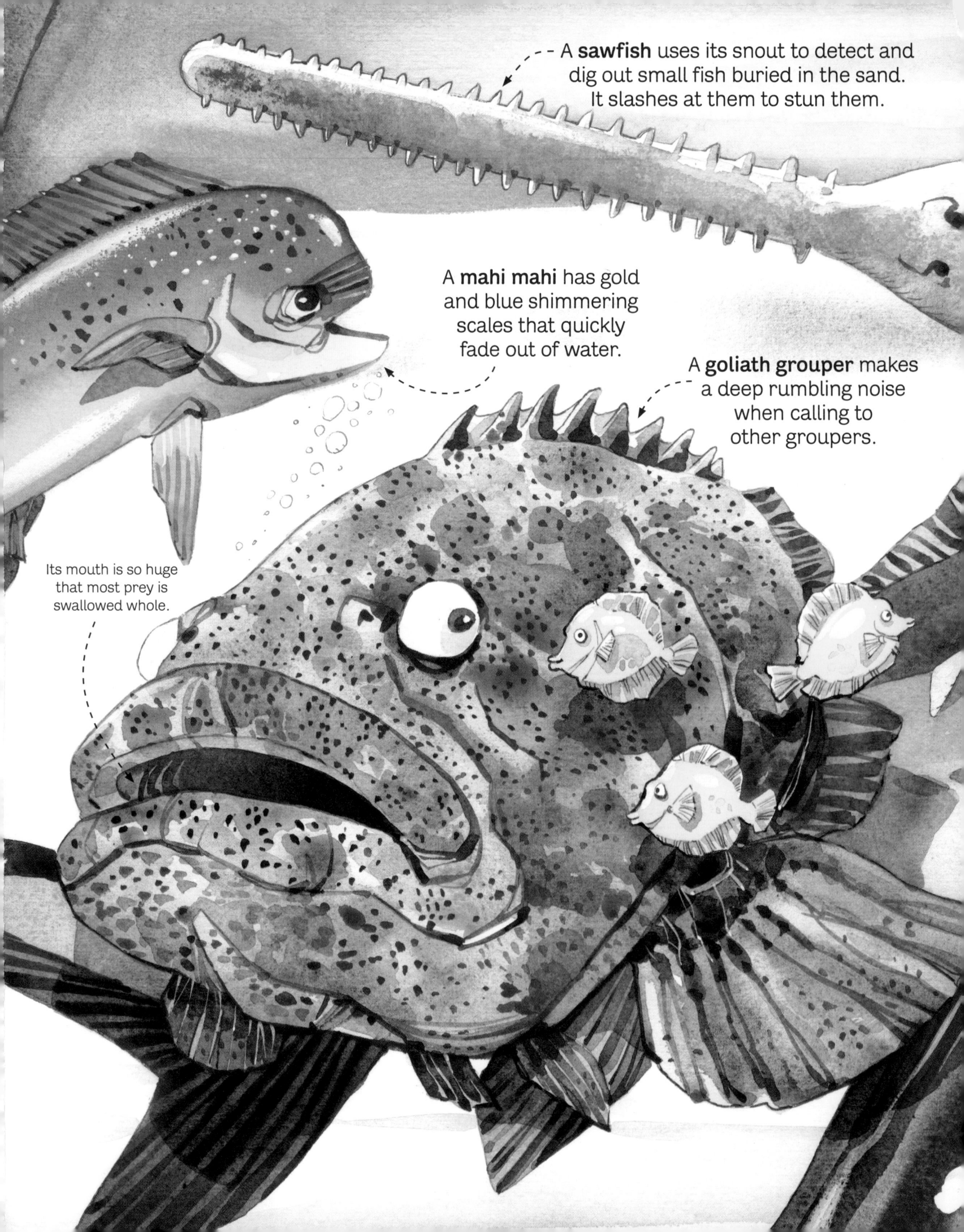
A **sawfish** uses its snout to detect and dig out small fish buried in the sand. It slashes at them to stun them.
A **mahi mahi** has gold and blue shimmering scales that quickly fade out of water.
A **goliath grouper** makes a deep rumbling noise when calling to other groupers.
Its mouth is so huge that most prey is swallowed whole.

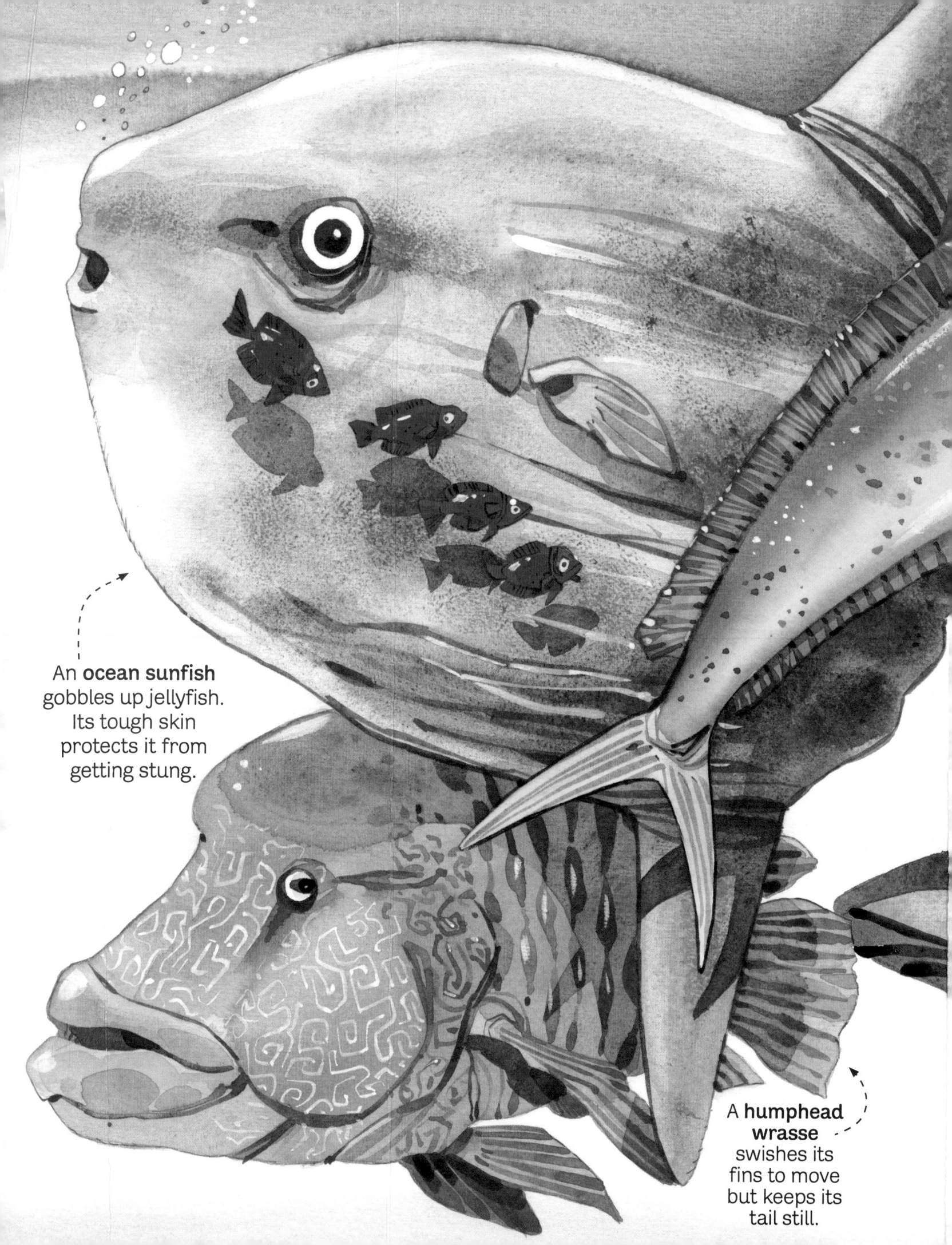

An **ocean sunfish** gobbles up jellyfish. Its tough skin protects it from getting stung.

A **humphead wrasse** swishes its fins to move but keeps its tail still.

Big fish

All fish breathe through gills at the sides of their heads. Most fish have a skeleton made of bone – except sharks and rays.

Mahi mahi have huge foreheads and long dorsal fins along their backs.
Length: up to 2m (6½ft)

Bluefin tuna are one of the fastest and biggest bony fish.
Length: up to 3m (10ft)

Humphead wrasse are some of the largest fish that live on coral reefs. They have a big bulge on their heads.
Length: up to 2m (6½ft)

Giant moray eels hide in rocky crevices during the day, and hunt at night.
Length: up to 2½m (8ft)

Swordfish are fast and acrobatic. They perform magnificent leaps out of the water.
Length: up to 4½m (15ft)

Ocean sunfish are the largest kind of bony fish. They often swim slowly near the surface.
Length: up to 3½m (12ft)

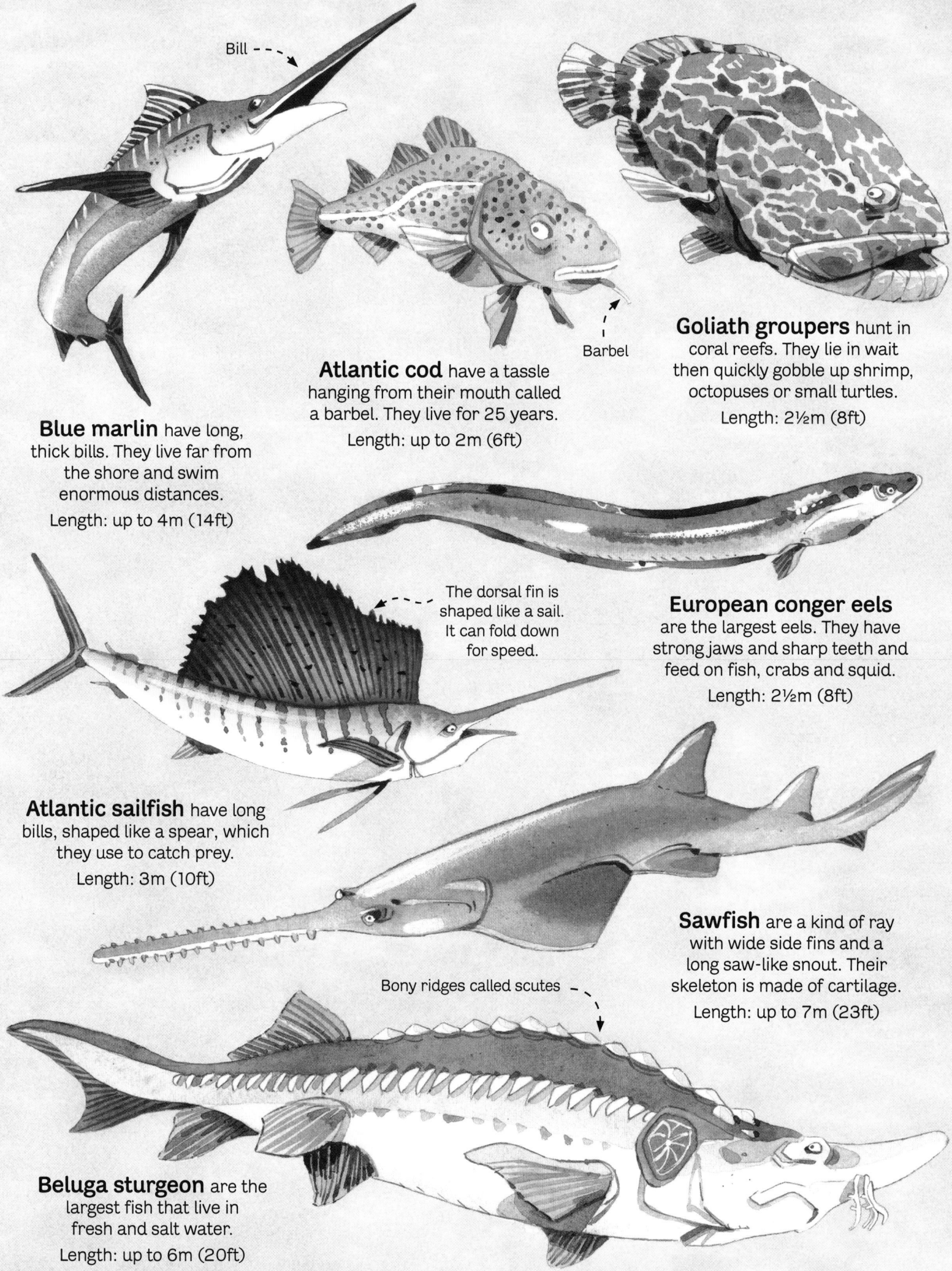

Blue marlin have long, thick bills. They live far from the shore and swim enormous distances.
Length: up to 4m (14ft)

Atlantic cod have a tassle hanging from their mouth called a barbel. They live for 25 years.
Length: up to 2m (6ft)

Goliath groupers hunt in coral reefs. They lie in wait then quickly gobble up shrimp, octopuses or small turtles.
Length: 2½m (8ft)

European conger eels are the largest eels. They have strong jaws and sharp teeth and feed on fish, crabs and squid.
Length: 2½m (8ft)

The dorsal fin is shaped like a sail. It can fold down for speed.

Atlantic sailfish have long bills, shaped like a spear, which they use to catch prey.
Length: 3m (10ft)

Sawfish are a kind of ray with wide side fins and a long saw-like snout. Their skeleton is made of cartilage.
Length: up to 7m (23ft)

Beluga sturgeon are the largest fish that live in fresh and salt water.
Length: up to 6m (20ft)

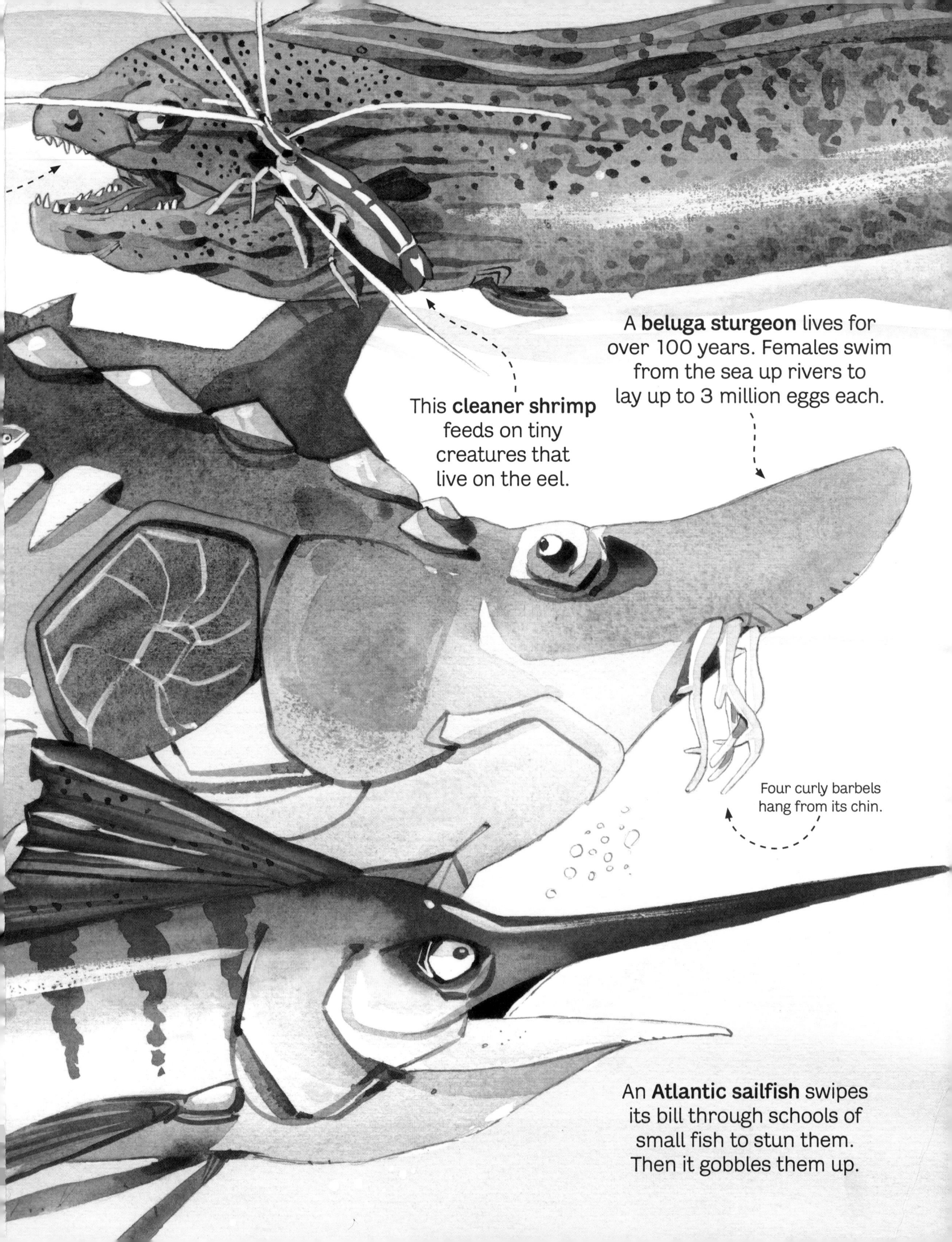
This **cleaner shrimp** feeds on tiny creatures that live on the eel.
A **beluga sturgeon** lives for over 100 years. Females swim from the sea up rivers to lay up to 3 million eggs each.
Four curly barbels hang from its chin.
An **Atlantic sailfish** swipes its bill through schools of small fish to stun them. Then it gobbles them up.

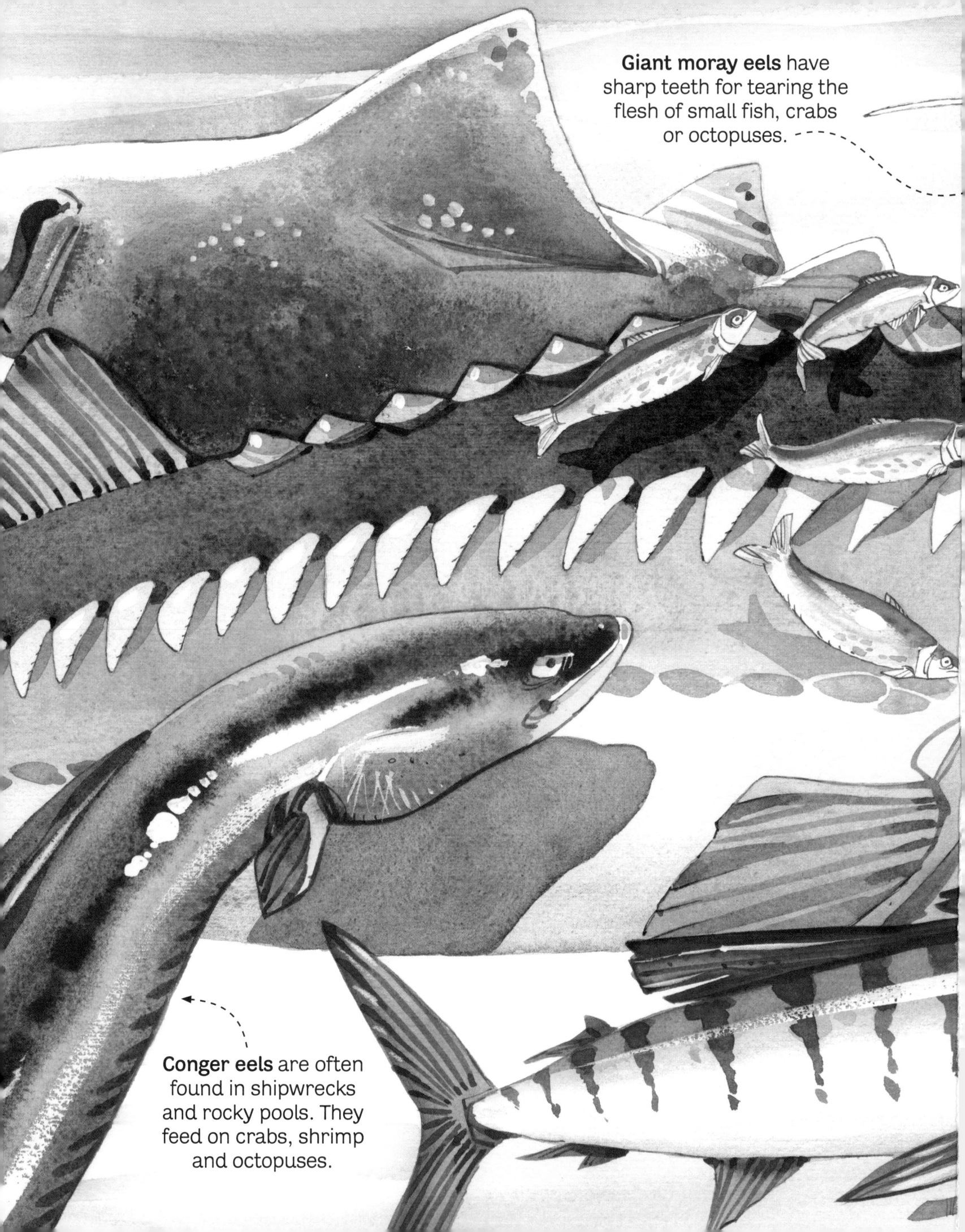
Giant moray eels have sharp teeth for tearing the flesh of small fish, crabs or octopuses.
Conger eels are often found in shipwrecks and rocky pools. They feed on crabs, shrimp and octopuses.

Biggest, fastest, longest...

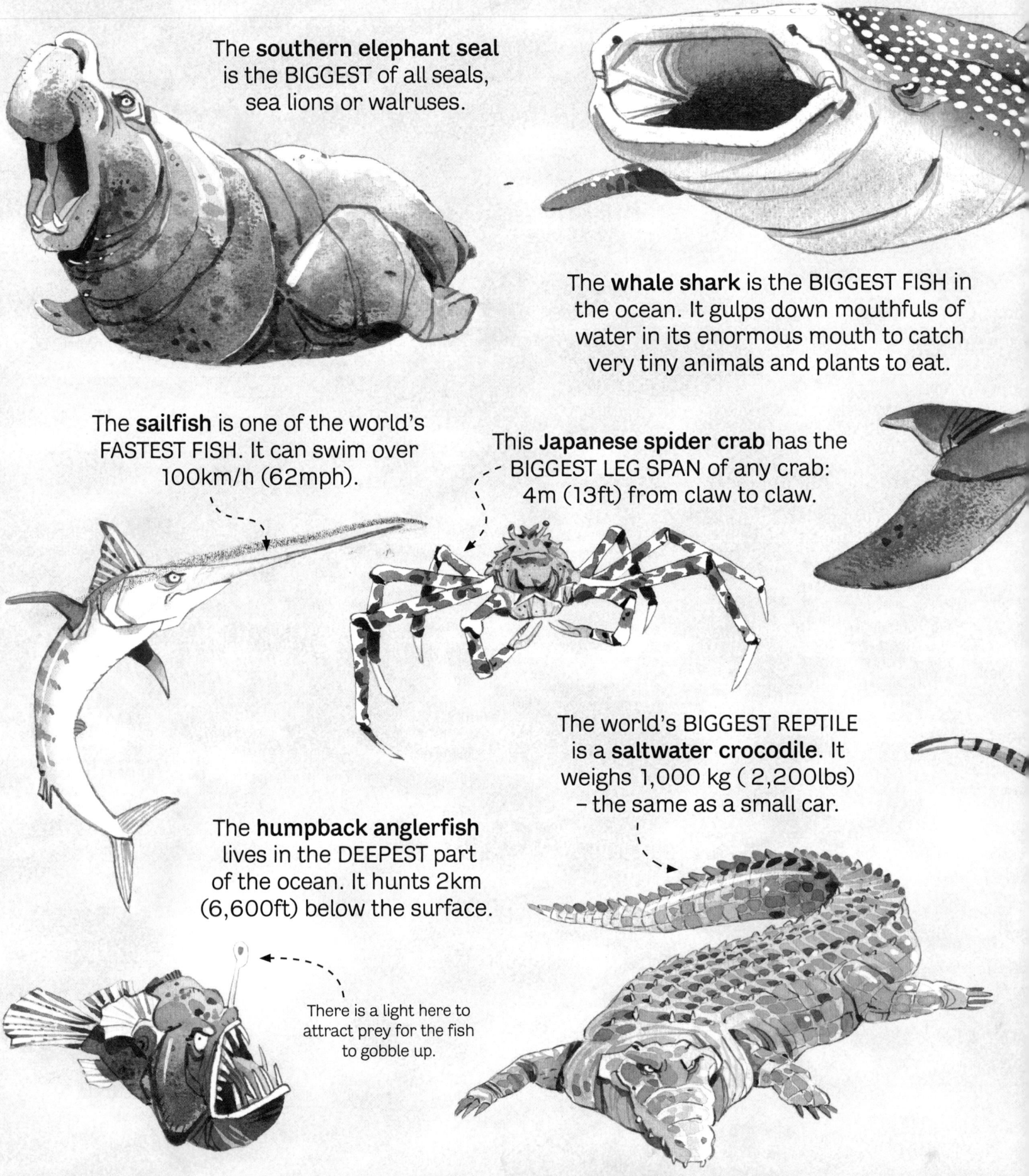

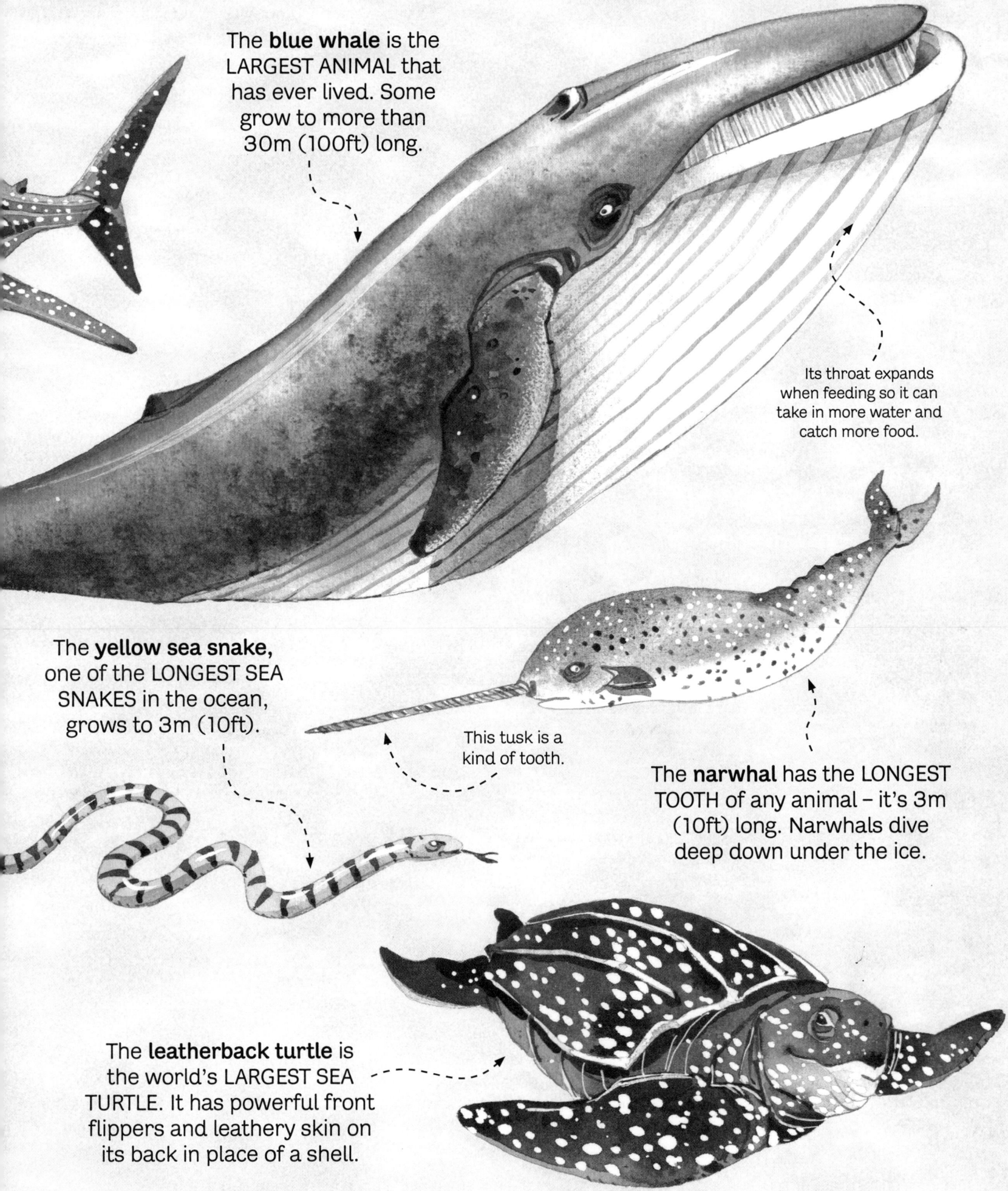
The **blue whale** is the LARGEST ANIMAL that has ever lived. Some grow to more than 30m (100ft) long.
Its throat expands when feeding so it can take in more water and catch more food.
The **yellow sea snake,** one of the LONGEST SEA SNAKES in the ocean, grows to 3m (10ft).
This tusk is a kind of tooth.
The **narwhal** has the LONGEST TOOTH of any animal – it's 3m (10ft) long. Narwhals dive deep down under the ice.
The **leatherback turtle** is the world's LARGEST SEA TURTLE. It has powerful front flippers and leathery skin on its back in place of a shell.

Series editor: Jane Chisholm
Additional design: Nelupa Hussain and Vickie Robinson
Image manipulation: Nick Wakeford and John Russell

This edition first published in 2016 by Usborne Publishing Ltd., Usborne House, 83-85 Saffron Hill, London EC1N 8RT, England. www.usborne.com Copyright © 2016, 2011 Usborne Publishing Ltd.

All rights reserved. No part of this publication may be reproduced, stored in a retrieval system or transmitted in any form or by any means, electronic, mechanical, photocopying, recording or otherwise, without the prior permission of the publisher. The name Usborne and the devices are Trade Marks of Usborne Publishing Ltd.
First published in America in 2012. Printed in China. UE.